Eric Brutnall is a primary school teacher living in Maidenhead, UK. He has been a teacher for eighteen years, working in the UK, Mexico and the Czech Republic.

Eric loves to travel and has been to many different places in the world, including Tanzania, Peru and Easter Island. He is inspired by stories for children and traditional myths told in different countries and cultures. *The Hope Star* is his first book.

THE HOPE STAR

Eric Brutnall

AUSTIN MACAULEY PUBLISHERS™
LONDON • CAMBRIDGE • NEW YORK • SHARJAH

A CIP catalogue record for this title is available from the British Library.

ISBN 9781788787680 (Paperback)
ISBN 9781788787864 (ePub e-book)

www.austinmacauley.com

First Published (2020)
Austin Macauley Publishers Ltd
25 Canada Square
Canary Wharf
London
E14 5LQ

For Andrew

There are lots of stories about the stars.
Where they come from.
What makes them shine.
Why they are there.
This is one of these stories.

When the universe began, energy was everywhere.
Energy created the galaxies.
It created the planets.
It created life.
Tiny pieces of this energy were left floating in space.
These fragments became the stars.

At the centre of every star was hope.
It flowed through them and shone from their very core; it was
their essence, their spirit, their soul.
For every act of kindness a star carried out,
it grew brighter and stronger.
A smile, a friendly word, a helping hand.
The universe became full of glittering stars; each one carrying out
kind deeds throughout space.

One of these stars was called Izar.
She was the brightest and kindest star.
Her brightness could be seen across the dark of space.
It was her dream to fill the universe with kindness.

Every day, Izar grew brighter as she carried out more and more
acts of kindness:
A smile, a friendly word, a helping hand.

In a corner of the universe, she noticed a beautiful planet, blue and green.
She would often wonder what it was like on that planet.
What made it so green and blue?
She dreamed of exploring it one day.
She kept returning to this wonderful planet of blue and green; each time getting closer and closer.

Then one day, she noticed that the colours were not as bright.
There was a greyness taking over the planet.
Izar watched, puzzled as the planet slowly lost its colour.
The blue and green drained away, leaving the planet dull and dark.

As she approached the planet, Izar could feel the dark and cold
that was covering the surface.
She landed and took a look around.
She was surrounded by a grey mist;
it covered everything like an icy blanket.

Izar looked closer.

She saw creatures and shadows walking around.

Each one had its head down – there was no contact between them.

There were no smiles, no laughter, no joy.

Izar realised that they had no hope!

Izar knew that she had to do something.

But how could she bring light to such a dark, grey place?

It was hope.
She had to spread hope across this planet, spread hope into each one of these sad, lonely figures.
She would have to share her own kindness, share her own hope.

Slowly, Izar started to carry out acts of kindness towards the shadowy figures:
A smile, a friendly word, a helping hand.

She could see the shadowy figures start to transform as the hope inside them began to grow.
The dark and grey melted away and they became filled with light.
She could see faces, hands and feet – they were people.
They began to smile, talk and help each other.

But with each act, instead of making her brighter, her own glow began to fade.
Izar started to feel cold and grey as her own hope left her.
She could feel her brightness disappear.
She looked at herself.
She was turning into a shadowy figure.

As she started to slip into shadow, Izar looked up.
She saw one of the figures standing over her.
It smiled down at her.
"Thank you," it said.
It reached out its hand and took hold of Izar's.
A smile, a friendly word, a helping hand.
An act of kindness!

A warmth swept through Izar as another figure approached. Then another, and another.
Soon she was surrounded by these former shadows – smiling at her, saying words of happiness, helping her to her feet.
They were all sharing their kindness with her, restoring her hope.

Izar felt herself fill up with hope once more.
She became brighter and brighter and started to float
up into the sky.
As she looked down, she saw the light of hope inside each person
chase away the darkness.
This light spread across the planet.
The blue and green returned once more.

Izar took her place back among the stars,
shining brightly and full of hope.
From time to time, she returned to the green and blue planet in the
corner of the universe.
The planet she gave hope to.
And maybe she would again.